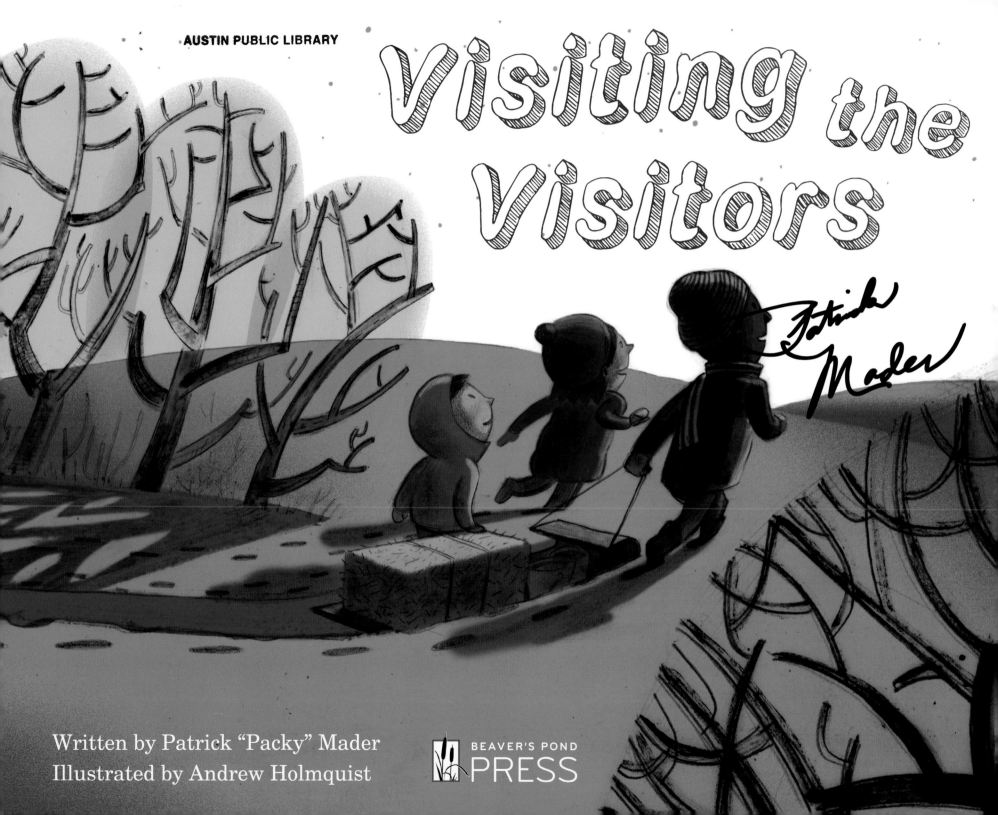

Visiting the Visitors

Written by Patrick "Packy" Mader

Illustrated by Andrew Holmquist

BEAVER'S POND
PRESS

ISBN: 978-1-59298-539-5
Library of Congress Control Number: 2012912234

Edited by Kellie Hultgren, KMH Editing
Project Manager, Amy Cutler Quale
Book design by Ryan Scheife, Mayfly Design
Typeset in New Century Schoolbook
The illustrations in this book were rendered with pencil, charcoal, graphite washes, colored pencil and marker and combined together in the computer with digital coloring.

Printed in the United States of America
First Printing: 2013

17   16   15   14   13   5   4   3   2   1

Beaver's Pond Press, Inc.
7108 Ohms Lane, Edina, MN 55439-2129
(952) 829-8818 • www.BeaversPondPress.com

To order, visit www.BeaversPondBooks.com or call (800) 901-3480.
Reseller discounts available.

Special thanks to Clete and Rosemary Speiker for welcoming visitors

To Greg and Rose (Doll) Mader,
Gerry and Karen (Krengel) Brandt,
and Jack Kennelly and Jeanette Mefford
Godparents extraordinaire
and
Karen, Karl, and Ellen
Wife, son, and daughter extraordinaire
—PM

To Sue, Chris, Matt, and Joshua
—AH

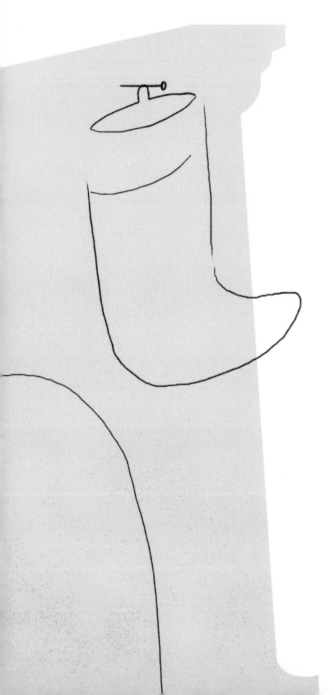

Grandma and Grandpa Farmer looked into the serious faces of their three grandchildren on a peaceful Christmas Eve night.

"Visit whom?" asked Grandma with a knowing smile.

"You know!" scolded the oldest grandchild, Malik. "We would like to visit the visitors again." The middle grandchild, Cassie, and the youngest grandchild, Balta, nodded their heads solemnly.

"Of course we should visit," Grandma and Grandpa agreed.

"Let's get dressed and take the sled for the gifts," added Grandpa. "It is a special holiday."

"Hooray!" cheered the three grandchildren as they dashed away to get their winter clothes.

The grandchildren bustled about as best they could while bundled in warm coats, hats, scarves, mittens, and boots.

They met Grandpa outside by the barn as he lifted a hay bale onto the sled. Malik and Cassie filled a small pail with corn and placed it on the sled too. And Balta smiled proudly as he tucked a handful of oats into his coat pocket.

Grandma looked at the clear, bright starry sky and announced, "It will
be easy to find the visitors tonight." She pointed to a gleaming star.
The grandchildren spotted it and knew the way would be well lit.

"Yes, and the visitors will be happy to see us!" exclaimed Cassie with awe and excitement. "Just like the baby and his parents were happy to see them."

Malik, Cassie, and Balta pulled on the rope tied to the loaded sled. They walked merrily along the path shown by the star.

Their footsteps fell deep into the soft snow, and the sled leveled a smooth path behind them. Grandma and Grandpa Farmer followed, still smiling.

Across a field they spied a small wooden stable. Inside the stable, three tall, robed wise men gazed down at a small child. The child's proud parents stood nearby.

Together the grandchildren pulled the sled close to the statues in the stable. Silent now, the three children stared at the scene.

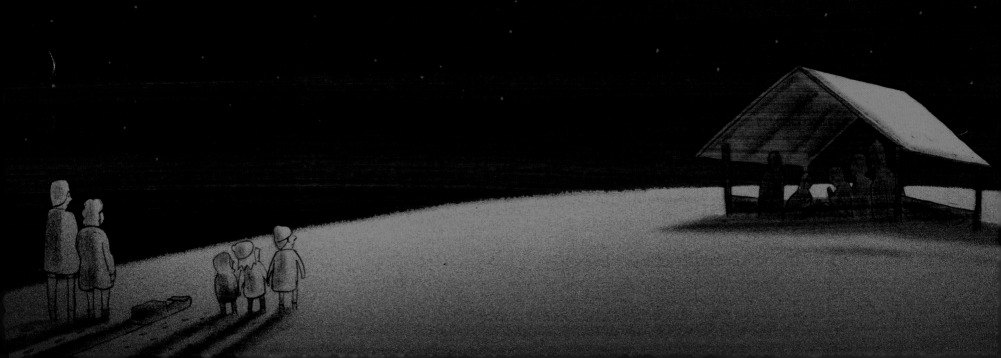

Slowly Malik approached the tallest statue. Then he took off his green scarf and wrapped it around the wise man and gave him a hug. "Thank you for visiting the child," Malik whispered.

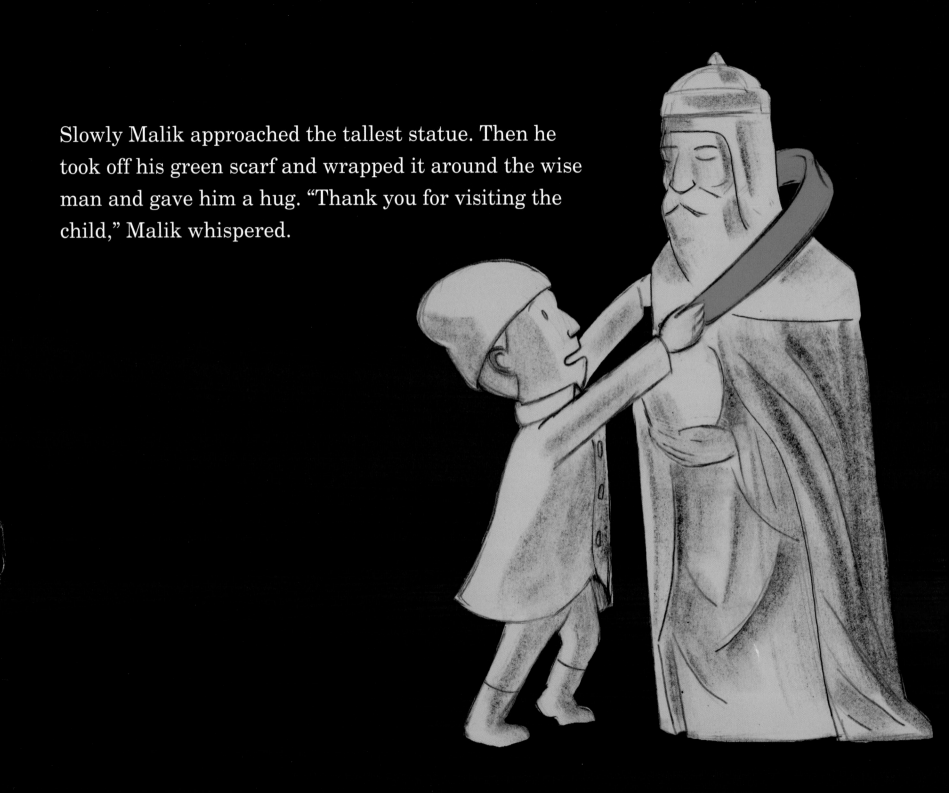

Then Cassie moved toward the next-tallest statue. Gently she placed her red hat on top of the second wise man's head and gave him a hug. "Thank you for visiting the family," Cassie whispered.

Finally Balta stepped close to the statue of a kneeling wise man. He tugged off his blue mittens, but he saw that they were too small for the third wise man's hands.

"What should I do?" asked Balta. "I would like to give my mittens to a visitor."

"We may have an answer in a minute," said Grandma. "Listen."

A bell tinkled. Out of the shadows of the stable stepped a cow, a donkey, and a lamb.

Then Grandpa lifted Balta over the donkey's head, and Balta saw the perfect place for his blue mittens. "Thank you for visiting everyone," Balta whispered into the donkey's warm ears.

Malik returned to the sled and brought the cow some hay. Cassie hauled the pail of corn over to the donkey.

Balta pulled oats from his coat pocket and
uncurled his fingers to let the lamb
nibble from his hand. It tickled.

Standing together in the calm of the holy night, everyone felt a magical silence in the air.

Grandma and Grandpa Farmer smiled as they looked at their grandchildren, the contented animals, the warm wise men, and the unmoving star high above.

Then the grandparents and the grandchildren all said to the wise men and the animals, "Thank you for the best visit ever."

Quietly they turned, looking at the still, snow-covered fields.

And they returned home by another path.

Patrick "Packy" Mader is an elementary teacher who lives in Northfield, Minnesota, with his wife and two children. *Visiting the Visitors* joins his other books, *Opa & Oma Together*, *Oma Finds a Miracle*, and *Big Brother Has Wheels!* as intergenerational stories that celebrate rural lifestyles.

Packy enjoys reading, traveling, and doing outdoor activities with friends and family. He also enjoys presenting programs to any interested group. The time and events around the holidays have a magical spirit to him.

For more information about his books and background, please visit **patrickmader.com**.

Andrew Holmquist is a painter and illustrator from Northfield, Minnesota. He is a graduate of the School of the Art Institute of Chicago and currently resides in Chicago, Illinois. Andrew has illustrated three other children's books and his paintings have been exhibited throughout the United States. For more information, please visit **andrewholmquist.com**.

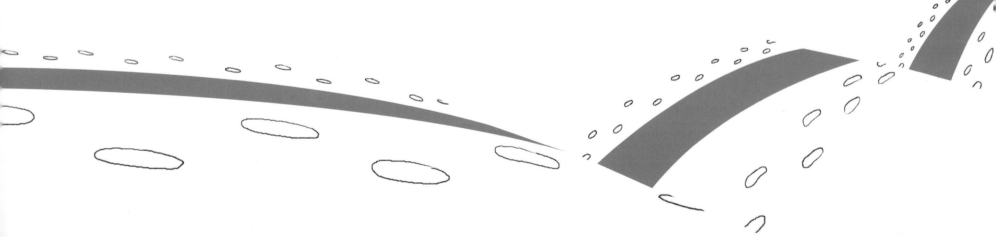